◇∇◇∇◇∇◇∇◇∇◇∇◇∇◇

Leo's world is full of **MONSTERS**, but his family, friends, and fellow villagers know nothing about that. What lies beyond the Village Wall is **TOP SECRET** and, as the **GUARDIAN'S APPRENTICE**, Leo has sworn to keep this secret safe.

Armed with a **SLINGSHOT**, pouch of **MAGICAL STONES**, and **MONSTER MAP**, it's Leo's job to keep his world in balance—protecting his village from the monsters that surround it.

◇∇◇∇◇∇◇∇◇

First American Edition 2022
Kane Miller, A Division of EDC Publishing

Text copyright © Kris Humphrey 2022
Illustrations copyright © Pete Williamson 2022
Leo's Map of Monsters: The Shrieking Serpent was originally
published in English in 2022. This edition is published by
arrangement with Oxford University Press.

For information contact:
Kane Miller, A Division of EDC Publishing
5402 S 122nd E Ave
Tulsa, OK 74146
www.kanemiller.com
www.myubam.com

Library of Congress Control Number: 2021948334

Printed and bound in the United States of America
1 2022

ISBN: 978-1-68464-488-9

LEO'S MAP OF MONSTERS

THE SHRIEKING SERPENT

KRIS HUMPHREY

ILLUSTRATED BY PETE WILLIAMSON

Kane Miller
A DIVISION OF EDC PUBLISHING

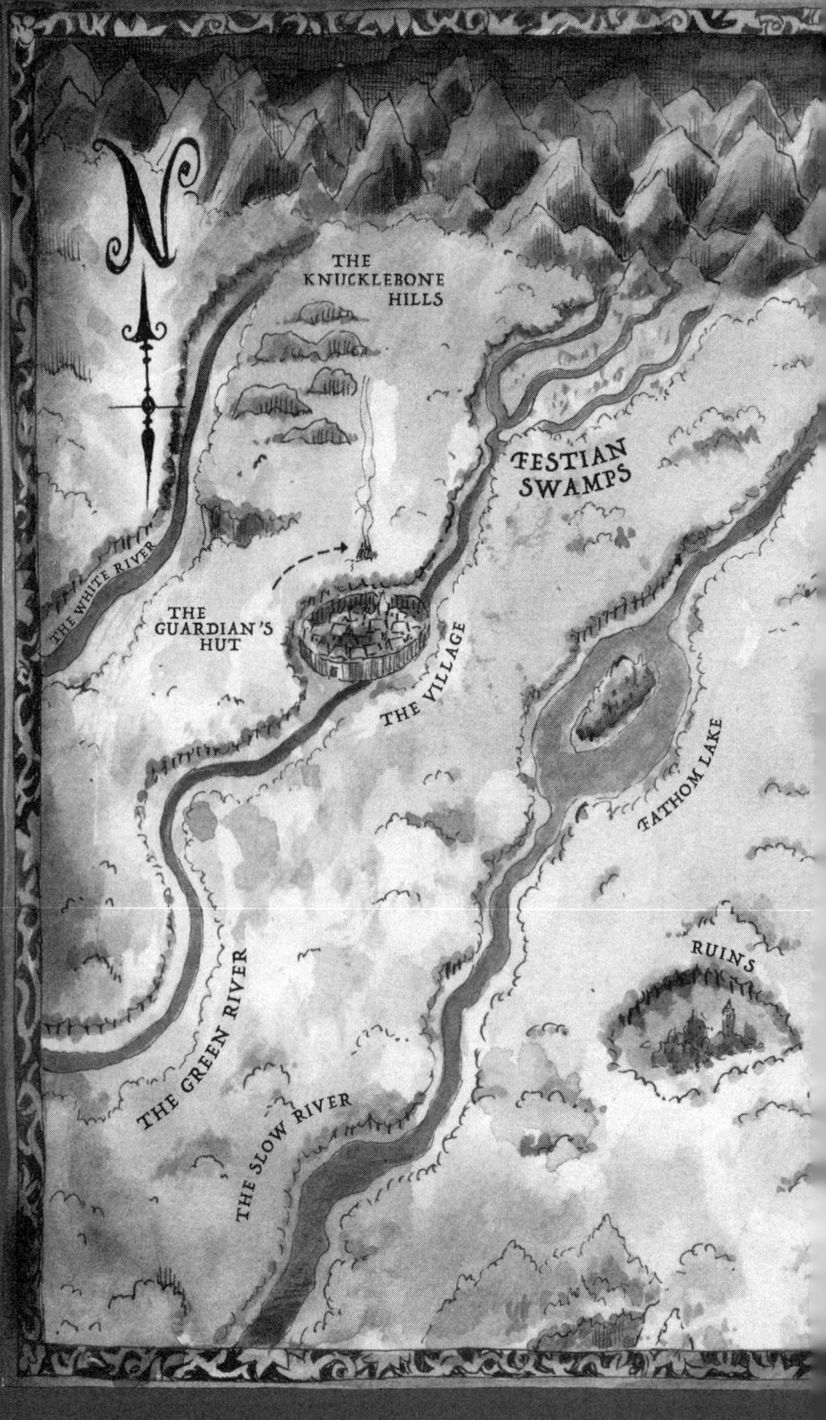

THE
KNUCKLEBONE
HILLS

FESTIAN
SWAMPS

THE WHITE RIVER

THE
GUARDIAN'S
HUT

THE VILLAGE

FATHOM LAKE

RUINS

THE GREEN RIVER

THE SLOW RIVER

NORTHERN
MOUNTAINS

CLAY
DESERT

THE EASTERN
RIVERS

EASTERN
PLAINS

MEET THE CHARACTERS

LEO: THE GUARDIAN'S APPRENTICE

GILDA: THE VILLAGE CHIEF

HENRIK: THE GUARDIAN

STARLA: LEO'S MONSTER FRIEND

EVE: LEO'S FRIEND

ONe

I lay in bed, staring at the wedge of daylight that had forced its way into my room. Outside, the village appeared to be waking up. Roosters crowed, shutters creaked, and cart wheels rumbled over the cobbled streets. It felt as if I'd only just gone to bed. How could it possibly be the morning already?

I sighed and threw the blanket off. Henrik wanted me to report to his cabin as early as possible, so there was no use trying to avoid the new day.

When I got downstairs, I found that Mum was already hard at work. A few weeks ago, she'd slipped in the street and injured her knee. My sister, Lulu, and I had moved her bed into the front room so that she didn't have to climb the stairs. Now Mum was propped up in bed, sorting a mass of papers into neat piles all around her.

She looked up and smiled.

"Morning, Leo!" she said.

"Morning," I grumbled, shuffling toward the kitchen.

To help out, Lulu and I were doing

more around the house than usual.
Breakfast was my job, so I shoved some
wood into the stove and got a fire going.
Then I filled the tea kettle and put
bread, jam, and butter on a tray.

"Oh, thanks, dear," Mum said when
I brought in the breakfast. "Sorry
about the mess. I've got to finish these
accounts today."

"Whose are they?" I asked, spreading some butter onto a slice of bread.

"The Grimwood family," Mum replied.

I must have frowned because when I looked up, Mum was watching me.

"I know the Grimwoods can be a little stern," she said, "but they pay well, and this is the only work I can do since I hurt my knee."

I nodded.

"It's a shame I don't get paid for doing my Assignment," I said.

"Well, yes," said Mum, "but you're helping in other ways."

She poured herself a cup of tea and held it up to illustrate her point.

As if she'd smelled the tea being poured, Lulu trudged down the stairs, yawning theatrically. Stickle the cat followed close behind her like a small, furry shadow.

"Thanks, Leo," she said, going straight for the tea.

She looked tired. Since Mum got injured, she'd been doing all the extra carpentry work she could find, and now that it was summer the long days meant she could keep working until late each evening.

"I've got an early start tomorrow," she said to Mum. "Footbridge repair down by the south wall. So I'll have to wait until my lunch break to deliver those papers to the Grimwoods."

My stomach tightened. I knew what was coming: if Lulu couldn't return the completed accounts then Mum would ask me to do it—and if I went anywhere near the Grimwood house I was sure to run into their oldest son, Carl Grimwood. I munched my bread and jam, keeping my eyes down as if I hadn't heard what Lulu just said.

"No problem, dear," Mum said to Lulu.

For a moment, I thought I'd gotten away with it. Maybe the Grimwoods wouldn't mind if their accounts were delivered late.

"You mustn't use up your lunch break," Mum went on. "Leo can drop the accounts back in the morning, can't you, Leo?"

I chewed on my bread and jam, finding that my appetite had suddenly vanished. Carl Grimwood was a bully. He was older than me and much bigger. Along with his idiot mates, his favorite hobby was tormenting anyone smaller than himself. Once they'd chased me and my best friend, Jacob, into Mrs. Kroner's goat pen. Then they'd pelted us with dung while we hid behind the angry goats, trying not to get kicked.

You were asking for trouble if you went anywhere near Carl Grimwood's

house, so if I knocked on the front door,
I wouldn't stand a chance.

But Mum was waiting for an answer.

"Uh-huh," I said, with my best attempt
at a smile. "I'll take the papers back in the
morning."

◂ ◊ △ ◊ ▸

As soon as I'd eaten, I set off across the village. I kept to the quiet backstreets, making sure I wasn't followed, and I soon reached the turnip man's warehouse and the secret door that led out of the village.

I still felt a thrill of danger every time I stepped out into the forest. I was an apprentice Guardian, and it was my job to make sure the monsters that roamed the forest never roamed too close to the village. It was also my job to keep the monsters a secret. Only three people knew the monsters existed: me, Henrik the Guardian, and Gilda, the Village Chief.

It had to stay that way to keep the villagers and the monsters safe.

Beyond the secret door I found the forest swaying gently in the early morning light. I set off, alert for signs of anything big or dangerous. Soon, all thoughts of Carl Grimwood had left my mind.

I followed a narrow path through the dense summer undergrowth and turned left at the tall stone marker that looked suspiciously like a giant tooth. Then I edged through the familiar tangle of thorns until the Guardian's ramshackle home emerged.

I wondered what Henrik had in

store for me. He'd probably found an especially dusty old book for me to study, or maybe the herb garden needed weeding again. We hadn't seen any monsters for a while, and I could tell he was trying to keep me busy. He'd even forced me to take swimming lessons in the freezing cold river. I shivered at the thought of it as I pushed open the cabin door.

"You took your time, boy," the Guardian muttered as I stepped inside.

He was sitting at his desk, polishing a small, shiny rectangle of metal.

"I had to make breakfast," I replied.

"Hmm," Henrik growled. "When I

was your age, I was hard at work before the sun was even up. No sleeping late. Definitely no breakfast."

He held the piece of metal up and angled it in the sunlight from the window. It glinted and shone, sending out a bright beam of reflected light.

"That'll have to do," he said, taking a rusty old lantern from the nearest shelf and slotting the polished piece of metal inside.

"What's that for?" I asked.

"It's for you," Henrik replied, fixing me with a serious look. "If you're lucky it'll keep you alive. Now come here, we can't afford to waste any more time."

I approached the desk, realizing this wasn't going to be a normal day after all.

"It's been a quiet few weeks," Henrik said. "And you've been doing well with your studying and your map practice . . ."

I gawped with surprise. It wasn't like Henrik to offer praise or encouragement.

". . . but the monsters won't stay away forever," he said. "And we've got ourselves a problem."

He opened his desk drawer and plucked out a limp piece of fabric, which I recognized immediately. It was the pouch where the magic stones were kept—and it was empty.

"No more stones," I muttered.

"That's right, boy. No more stones."

Since the start of my Assignment the slingshot and stones had been the only protection I'd had against the monsters. The stones were precious objects, full of strange powers, and I'd done my best not to waste them. The trouble was, my aim with the slingshot hadn't always been that good.

"I didn't think we'd run out so fast," said Henrik. "And I couldn't send you to get more until I knew you were ready."

"So you think I'm ready?" I asked hopefully.

"Well . . ." said Henrik. "We'll soon find out."

He fixed me with a narrow-eyed stare. Then he produced a rectangle of worn, waxy paper from his drawer and began unfolding it on the desk. Colored lights moved across its surface, a vast assortment of tiny, illuminated shapes, each representing a monster.

I stepped closer and gazed down at the Map of Monsters.

"Here," said Henrik, planting a finger near the top of the map.

"The Northern Mountains?" I said. "But they're miles away. And there's snow and rocks and . . . have you seen how tall they are?"

"What did you expect, boy? They don't sell magic stones in the village shop."

I pictured the vast, jagged peaks that rose above the forest.

"But I don't think I can climb a mountain," I said, staring blankly at the map.

"No need for climbing," Henrik

growled. "The stones are inside. In the
Endless Mines."

I looked up at Henrik. He had to be
joking.

But Henrik didn't joke. He nodded
back at me in grim silence.

I'd read about the Endless Mines. They'd been carved from the rock beneath Mammoth Peak, so long ago that no one knew who had done it. It was a pitch-dark labyrinth, countless miles of tunnels crossed by underground rivers. A habitat that even the nastiest varieties of rock monsters avoided.

Henrik must have seen how scared I was because he softened his voice when he spoke.

"It's a tough job," he said. "But it has to be done. And I'm too old to do it. You know we can't protect the village without a fresh supply of stones. So just think about your family and friends. That'll help you along."

"But how am I supposed to get all the way through the forest without any stones?" I asked. "I'll have nothing to defend myself with."

"Well, that's not true," Henrik replied. "You have this."

He tapped a bony finger against my forehead.

"You've got a brain in there somewhere, boy, and you've been studying the monsters and the forest for a good while now. You'll have the map to help you, too—and that Leatherwing friend of yours."

He was talking about Starla, the small

flying monster who'd joined me on all my missions so far. The thought of having her by my side made me feel slightly better. Unfortunately, that feeling didn't last very long.

"There's one more thing you need to know," Henrik said, pointing to a gray, arrow shape lurking deep within Mammoth Peak.

"That," he said, "is the Shrieking Serpent."

I stared at Henrik, then shook my head, unwilling to believe what I was hearing.

"But the Shrieking Serpent doesn't exist," I said. "The books say it's just a myth. No one's ever seen it."

"A long time has passed since those books were written," Henrik replied. "Things change. Monsters move from place to place. I don't know where it came from, but I know it's there because I've seen it with my own eyes."

"You've actually seen it?" I asked.

Henrik nodded slowly.

"Ten years ago," he said. "The last time I entered the mines to gather magic stones. It was there and it almost got the better of me."

"But how did you escape?" I asked.

"I was lucky," Henrik said. "And I did have one last handful of magic stones with me. But mostly it was luck, boy."

He shook his head as if the memory of that narrow escape was too disturbing to think about.

According to the legends, the Shrieking Serpent was longer than a tree is tall, and faster than the wind. It hunted in the dark using high-pitched shrieks, studying the echoes like a bat. Its sight and hearing were so sensitive to movement that no living thing could pass by unnoticed.

I felt a cold knot of dread inside me.

"But I won't have any stones," I said. "And what if I'm not as lucky as you?"

"You'll have a couple of things I didn't

have," the Guardian replied, sliding the rusty old lantern toward me across the desk. The metal plate he'd been polishing reflected a rainbow of colors from the lights on the map. "This'll cast a strong beam straight ahead," Henrik said. "So you'll be able to find your way through the tunnels. And this is a plan of the mines."

He produced a small hand-drawn map and placed it on the table. It was an intricate network of thin black lines, with one blue line passing through the center.

"Use it to avoid the Serpent," he said, "but if it gets close, there's one last thing that might help."

He held out a tiny bottle in the palm of his hand. Inside was a silvery powder.

"Remember the show I put on at Spring Festival?" he asked me.

"Of course," I said.

People were still talking about the mysterious, hooded Fire Mage who'd turned the bonfire every color imaginable and sent its flames towering above the rooftops.

"This is one of the powders I used," said Henrik. "It's strong stuff and it'll burn so bright the Serpent will be blinded—none of its senses will work. The effect isn't permanent, but it should last long enough for you to get away."

He handed me the bottle and began assembling the other things I would need:

a tinderbox, spare oil for the lantern, a flask of water, and some food. He packed them all into a knapsack.

"One last thing," he said to me, gesturing toward the map he'd drawn. "You see this blue line?"

I looked closely.

"The one running north to south?" I asked.

"That's an underground river," Henrik said. He pointed to where the river crossed one of the tunnels marked in black. "Here, in a big cavern, you'll find a waterfall." He looked up at me. "You'll have to dive into the pool directly beneath it. That's where you'll find the stones."

I stared at the tiny blue line and imagined how cold the water would be.

"It's a long walk to the mines," said Henrik. "So you won't be home before nightfall. Gilda will let your mother know."

Then he handed me both maps. The look he gave me was grave but softened by a kind of encouragement I'd never seen in him before.

"Time to go, lad."

TWo

I set off through the forest, checking

the map constantly as I made my way

toward the Green River. My plan

was to follow the river

north, all the way to the

Festian Swamps, which

lay directly below

Mammoth Peak.

Then I'd search for

the entrance to the Endless Mines.

I hurried through the trees, afraid I might bump into a monster when I had no magic stones to protect myself. I could see from the map that a pair of Grass Gulpers were feeding on the far side of the river. There was a small Mud Kraken sleeping in the silty riverbed too. Further north, the usual herds of Armored Goretusks were wallowing about in the Festian Swamps.

Soon I heard the gurgling of the river and I emerged into one of the small grassy meadows that clung to its banks. The summer sun washed over me, and it felt good to be out of the trees for a while.

I headed north along the river path and squinted into the far distance, at the immense, craggy outline of Mammoth Peak.

As I stared, I noticed a small dark speck gliding through the air. It appeared to be getting bigger. I studied the map and saw a small amber light shooting downriver toward me. It was a Leatherwing. I smiled and lowered the map. There was only one Leatherwing in the forest.

"Starla!" I called as she swooped into the clearing.

"Leo Wilder!" she replied, her voice arriving directly inside my head in that strange, echoey way of hers.

She hovered in front of me, batting the air with her big black wings. Her forked tail flicked about excitedly.

"Where have you been, Leo Wilder?" she asked. "I haven't seen you for ages!"

"I know," I said, realizing just how much I'd missed her. "I was studying and training the whole time, and Henrik even made me learn to swim."

"Yuck!" said Starla. "Water is not a good place at all. Always so wet and never staying still and it makes your fur so heavy that you can't even fly . . ."

I laughed as she shook her head in disgust.

"I was hoping I'd bump into you," I said, setting off along the riverside path.

Starla flew beside me.

"I have a new mission," I said. "Maybe you'd like to come with me?"

"Yes, of course!"

She flapped about merrily, then flew backward so we were face-to-face while I walked.

"So where are we going?" she asked. "What misbehaving monster are we searching for?"

"We're going to the Endless Mines," I said.

Starla grew very serious all of a sudden. "Oh," she said. "Oh dear."

She flew alongside me in silence for a while and I could tell she was scared, which made me feel even more nervous about the mission. But soon Starla was back to her usual impatient self, swooping back and forth, scouting out the path ahead, and telling me to hurry up.

I walked as fast as I could, but the path was getting steeper and rockier all the time. I had to watch where I was putting my feet, which meant I couldn't check the map very often, and I kept imagining all the monsters creeping about in the surrounding forest.

Somehow, we reached the edge of the Festian Swamps without getting eaten, and I stopped to catch my breath. I'd been here once before, on my very first job as apprentice Guardian, when I'd led a young Armored Goretusk back here to find its herd. It was the furthest north I'd ever been.

I could see a group of Goretusks now, rising from the steaming swampland like rock-encrusted islands. They were huge four-legged creatures with crooked horns that sprouted from the sides of their heads. Although they could be incredibly fierce, all they really wanted to do was wade about in the swamp and

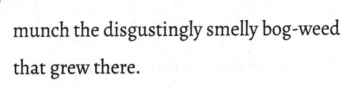

munch the disgustingly smelly bog-weed
that grew there.

Mammoth Peak was much closer now,
and without the forest all around us I

could see the foothills and rocky slopes that formed its base.

Starla flapped down and perched beside me on a moldy tree stump.

"The mines are not far," she said. "But you need to be careful in these stinking swamps. Your legs will stick in the mud very easily, Leo Wilder. Wait here and I'll find a path for you."

I took off my knapsack and laid it at my feet, watching as Starla rose into the bright morning sky. I gazed across at the menacing bulk of the mountain. Somewhere inside all that rock was a pool full of magic stones, guarded by a monster so deadly it was thought to be a myth. I felt a strong urge to turn around and go home, to try spending my days doing something less dangerous. I could work for the turnip man, or learn to milk goats, or I could train as a dung shoveler . . .

I was so absorbed in these thoughts that I didn't hear the charging Goretusk until it was too late.

There was a roar and a heavy splash of feet behind me. I turned and glimpsed a snorting mass of fur and horns. Then the monster hit me in the chest, and I flew off my feet, landing in the swamp with a thumping splash. I stared up at the huge, flared nostrils of the monster, then the cold, stinking swamp water closed over my face. I tried to push myself up, but my hands and feet only sank deeper. I was being sucked into the mud below.

THREE

I reached out desperately and caught hold of something solid. Using all my strength, I managed to pull my head out of the water.

I gasped for air and dragged myself up so I was sitting in the mud. The surface of the swamp rippled around my chest and foul-smelling swamp water clung to my face and blurred my vision. I felt the mud beneath me trying to suck me back down every time I moved, so I kept a firm grip on the solid object in my hand. Eventually, the water drained from my face and I could see again.

The object I was holding was long and curved. At one end it was sharply pointed and at the other it was attached to the wide, drooling face of the Goretusk that had attacked me.

I stared into the monster's eyes and knew that there was nothing I could do. I was stuck, completely at its mercy. It was twenty times my size and it could crush me or drown me or chew me up if it wanted to. I was frozen with fear. I didn't even think to let go of its tusk.

The Goretusk snorted in my face and its rotten breath ruffled my hair.

From a distance I could hear Starla's wings as she flapped toward me.

"It's all right!" she cried. "Don't worry!"

I couldn't see how she could help me, but a moment later I understood what she meant.

Instead of attacking me, the Goretusk
moved gently backward, drawing me
up out of the water as I held tight to its
tusk. I rose to my feet, lifted easily by its
extraordinary strength.

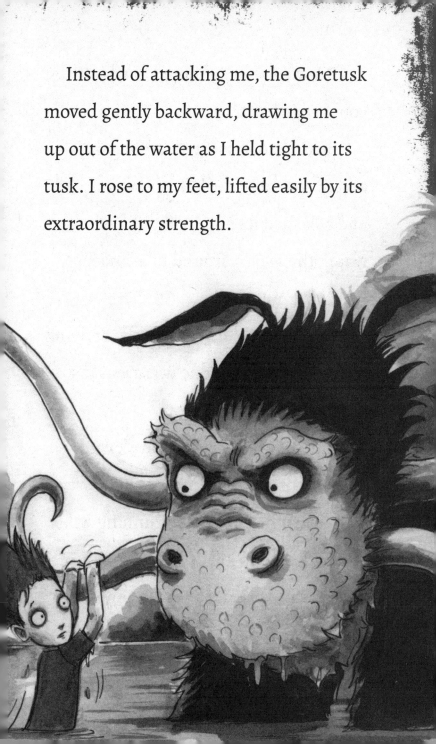

"Don't you see?" shouted Starla. "Don't you recognize it?"

The Goretusk snorted once again, and I let go of its tusk. It shook its head and splashed its huge, clawed feet in the water, then spun around in a circle.

"Oh!" I muttered.

"Yes, Leo Wilder," said Starla, arriving by my side. "It's the one we saved. It's our friend!"

This was the young Goretusk we'd tracked through the forest on my very first mission. It had been running wild and had tried to kill us both a couple of times. But I'd found a Hawkupine quill stuck in its leg and after we'd removed it the Goretusk had been much more friendly.

The huge monster leaned toward me and nudged me playfully with its nose. I laughed as I realized it must have recognized me and Starla right away.

It had just wanted to say hello.

"I need to get out of this swamp," I said to Starla.

But when I tried to walk back to dry land I found that my feet were completely stuck in the mud.

"I told you to stay on the path, Leo Wilder," said Starla. "This swamp mud is dangerous."

"Well, I didn't have much choice," I muttered, trying with all my strength to lift my feet out of the mud. "You try staying on the path when an Armored Goretusk bashes into you."

The Goretusk watched me as I struggled in the mud, knee-deep in stagnant water.

Then a low, mournful booming sound echoed round the swamps and the monster turned its head. It gave me one last friendly snort before it splashed away. It had been called back to the herd.

"Well, I'm glad it was pleased to see us, but what am I supposed to do now?" I said.

Starla was hovering in front of me, not paying much attention. Instead, she was peering back across the swamp toward the forest.

"Do you see that?" she asked me.

Her tail swished nervously as I scanned the trees at the southern edge of the swamp.

"See what?" I replied.

"We are being watched, Leo Wilder. Let me find out what is doing the watching."

And she flew high into the air, before circling south and diving into the forest.

I looked around, feeling very stuck and very exposed. The Map of Monsters would have been useful, but it was in my knapsack, out of reach over on the path. I was about to call out to Starla when a

movement caught my eye.

I stared toward the forest, hoping it was her.

Instead, I saw a small group of people emerging from the trees.

Their clothes were forest colors, every imaginable shade of green, and they each carried either a spear or a bow. They moved in silence round the edge of the swamp, and I watched nervously as they approached.

FoUR

They were forest people, and they did
not look friendly. I'd only met forest
people once before: a girl called Eve who
was about my age, and her little sister,
Willow. We'd battled a pair of Spitfang
Lizards together, and then the girls had
vanished back into the forest without
saying goodbye.

The group stalking toward me now

did not contain Eve or Willow. There were five of them and they were all grown-ups. They were led by a young woman who carried a bow and arrow. Her weapon was aimed at the ground, but the string was pulled tight, and it looked ready to fire at a moment's notice. She scanned her surroundings as she walked and all five of them moved carefully but confidently along the edge of the swamp. There was no sign of Starla, and I hoped she was out of range of the bows.

"What's your name?" the leader called to me as she drew near.

"Leo," I said. "I'm stuck."

"I can see that," she said. "My name's Wynter. I don't recognize you. What camp are you from?"

"I'm not from a camp," I said. "I'm from the village."

She frowned at me.

"You're a long way from home," she said. "I thought you villagers were too scared to step out from behind your wall?"

"Not all of us," I said. "I'm heading to Mammoth Peak and the Endless Mines."

"Did you hear that?" a man with a spear said. "He's heading for the Endless Mines."

He let out a burst of laughter and a few of the others laughed, too.

Wynter just watched me suspiciously.

"The mines are no place for the likes of you," she said. "Neither is the forest. You obviously can't look after yourself." She turned to one of her people. "Throw him a rope and get him out of there."

They quickly dragged me out of the swamp and onto dry land. My boots were caked in mud and my shirt was gooey with Goretusk snot.

"Thanks for unsticking me," I said, "but I really do have to get going."

"No," said Wynter. "You're coming with us."

"But I have to get to the mines . . ." I said.

Wynter silenced me with a shake of her head. The look she gave me was cold and hard. She was deadly serious.

I looked around at the rest of Wynter's gang and was met with stony stares and mocking smiles. Fingers flexed on the grips of weapons and I could tell it wasn't worth arguing with these people. So I nodded and let them lead me back toward the trees.

We walked in single file down paths I never would have seen. Wynter led the way, watching the trees and keeping her bow and arrow drawn. I was painfully aware of how noisy my squelching, clumsy footsteps were. No one else seemed to make a sound.

Soon the smell of wood smoke drifted through the trees and I heard the echo of voices and the rhythmic thud of an axe. I hoped that when we reached the camp, I'd have the chance to explain myself. It was past midday already, and I should have been in the foothills of the mountain by now.

We passed a pair of guards armed with spears, then we arrived in the camp of the forest people.

Circular tents were scattered through the trees. Some had smoke drifting from openings in their roofs. Others had stone-ringed firepits outside. The people of the camp wore the same loose, forest-colored clothing as Wynter and her group. They all seemed to be hard at work: weaving or chopping, polishing weapons, or mending clothes. The ones who saw me looked up from their work with a mixture of curiosity and suspicion.

We arrived at an area of open ground

that seemed to be the center of the camp.
People sat on blankets or perched on logs
all around its edge. Clothes and weapons
were being bought and sold, and there
were several small fires with bubbling

pots of food hanging over them.

At the far end stood a tent that was much bigger than the others. Its green fabric was strung with garlands of flowers and ropes of woven vines.

"I'll see if Crow wants a look at him," said Wynter, disappearing into the tent and leaving the rest of us to wait outside.

I stared around at the camp, wondering if Eve and Willow were here. I also wondered how these people managed to survive out here among the monsters. They looked tough. Everyone was working, even the young children and the very old. I watched an elderly man whittling the shaft of an arrow. He checked that it was straight, then dropped it into a pile of others at his feet. He looked up at me and stared for a moment before giving me a short, friendly nod. I nodded back as I heard Wynter emerge from the tent behind me.

"Come on," she said. "Crow's waiting."

Flames crackled inside the tent and the air was smoky. It took a moment for my eyes to adjust, then I saw a large central fire surrounded by huddles of people. They whispered to each other as I passed, their faces flickering with light and shadow. I looked back and saw the tent flap sway as more of the forest people followed us inside.

Beyond the fire there was a raised platform covered with blankets of all different colors. A man sat cross-legged on the platform, and his sparkling eyes watched me intently as I was led toward him.

"So this is the village boy," he said.

The tent fell silent.

I peered through the gloom and saw that the man, Crow, was about Henrik's age. He had broad shoulders and long, dark hair. His jaw was heavily scarred on one side.

"And he was heading for the Endless Mines?" Crow asked.

"That's what he claims," Wynter replied.

"It's the truth," I said. "Henrik, our town Guardian, sent me to the mines on an important mission. I'm his apprentice."

A low murmur swept through the room and there was some shuffling of feet.

I felt the force of Crow's piercing gaze as he considered what I'd said.

"Henrik . . ." the old man muttered. A sour expression passed across his face.

"A boy like this would never be trusted with such a task," Wynter said. "We found him stuck in the Festian Swamps. He would have starved or been eaten alive by Swooper Birds if we hadn't saved him."

Crow narrowed his eyes at me, but he seemed thoughtful rather than angry.

"Why would Henrik send a defenseless boy on such a dangerous journey?" he mused.

"He wouldn't," said Wynter. "Nobody would. The boy's making it all up. He's a runaway and he's causing trouble for us. We need to send him back to the village."

She gave me an unpleasant look and I scowled back at her.

"I'm telling the truth," I said to Crow. "Henrik's too old to travel so far, so he sent me instead."

"And what exactly is Henrik so desperate to take from the mines?" Crow replied.

"Stones," I replied hesitantly. "The magic ones we use to ward off the monsters."

The tent came alive with frantic whispering and Crow's eyes widened for a moment. I wondered how much these people knew about the village and the magic stones. Perhaps these things were as strange and secret to them as the forest people were to me.

"Quiet," Crow said softly. "Please."

The tent grew still and silent once again. Crow studied me with his bright, sharp eyes. I tried to stand tall and look like a genuine apprentice Guardian, which was harder than usual thanks to all the swamp mud and Goretusk snot on my clothes.

"Magic stones," murmured Crow, almost to himself. "And the boy says they come from the Endless Mines?"

"He's obviously lying," Wynter insisted. "Let me take him back to his village and . . ."

"Thank you, Wynter," Crow interrupted.

Wynter nodded respectfully, but I could see she was angry and embarrassed.

The tent was quiet for a moment. Then somebody called out:

"Crow, I think he's telling the truth!"

I turned and saw the crowd of forest people that had gathered beyond the fire.

At the front of the crowd was a face I instantly recognized. It was Eve.

"I've met him before," she said. "He *is* an apprentice Guardian and . . ."

Eve paused, as if deciding whether to go on.

"He . . . he used one of his stones to help me and Willow fight a Spitfang Lizard, over in the Knucklebone Hills. If he says there are magic stones in the mines, then he's probably right."

All around her, the people of the camp muttered and shook their heads. I smiled at her and she nodded back nervously. I felt a wave of gratitude toward her.

"I can go with him," Eve went on. "If you're worried he'll get hurt. I can help him get to the mines and back home to his village."

Beside me, Wynter shook her head and laughed.

"Since when did we risk our lives helping villagers with their unnatural magical stones?" she said.

All around the tent, others joined in with disapproving shouts.

"I don't need your help!" I insisted. "I can get to the mines by myself!"

But my voice was drowned out by all the others.

"Silence!" Crow bellowed, rising to

his feet. He was tall and powerful, and I instinctively shrank back as he towered over me.

His voice echoed round the tent and his people bowed their heads.

"This forest is no place for childish games," he said. "If there are magic stones inside the mines, then they should stay there. The boy will be fed, and he will rest, and at first light tomorrow Wynter will return him to his village."

He turned to Wynter.

"Find a space for him to sleep," he said, "and make sure he stays there until morning."

"Yes," she said, placing a hand on my shoulder and pulling me away.

The crowd parted around us and I searched for Eve in the flickering light. But she was nowhere to be seen.

FIVe

Night fell but it was impossible to sleep. I'd been shut inside some kind of storage tent, which was crammed with old pots and pans and odd-shaped bundles of fabric that didn't smell very nice. My clothes didn't smell too good either. The swamp water and Goretusk snot had dried into a hard crust that made things even more uncomfortable. All I'd been given to sleep on was a blanket, and I sat with it wrapped around my shoulders while I stared at the Map of Monsters with tired eyes.

I could see the Goretusks nearby in the swamps and a flock of Swooper Birds further away to the west. I quickly spotted Starla's small amber light, too.

She wasn't far away, but she was scared of the forest people and I knew she wouldn't dare approach the camp. Again and again, I checked the area around the village. I should have been home by now with a fresh supply of stones. There were no monsters nearby, but that could change in an instant and I wouldn't be around to help.

I needed to get out of the camp, but escape seemed impossible. Wynter was right outside and when I'd tested the knots that sealed the tent flap, I'd received a sharp jab in the ribs with the butt of a spear.

"Don't even think about it, village boy,"

Wynter had snapped at me.

So I sat there, huddled miserably inside my blanket. I thought about Mum and Lulu, knowing they'd be up all night worried sick about me. I probably wouldn't even be back in time to take the accounts to the Grimwoods like I'd promised. Lulu would end up doing it.

I realized I was glad not to have to face Carl Grimwood. But I immediately felt a twist of guilt in my stomach. Worse still, I felt a sense of powerlessness settle over me. I was an apprentice Guardian, I'd fought deadly monsters all over the forest, but I still couldn't stand up to people like Carl Grimwood or Wynter.

The night wore on and I anxiously watched the colored monster lights moving across the map. Eventually, my eyes began to close, and my head drooped onto my chest. I tucked the map away beneath the blanket and fell into a restless sleep.

A hand on my shoulder was the first thing I remember. Then a harsh whisper in my ear:

"Wake up!"

I scrambled to my feet, peering frantically around the pitch-black tent.

"Who's there?" I demanded.

"Quiet!" hissed the voice. "It's me, Eve. I've come to get you out of here."

As my eyes adjusted, I saw a crouching

shadow near the back of the tent.

"Come on," she whispered. "We have to go now."

I stood for a moment, feeling stunned and drowsy. Then my thoughts cleared. Eve was helping me. This was my way out.

I slipped the map into my knapsack and shook the blanket off my shoulders.

"All right," I said. "Let's go."

Eve pulled open a crooked flap of canvas that she must have cut herself.

"What about Wynter?" I whispered.

"She's asleep," Eve hissed. "You'll wake her up if you keep talking. Just go!"

I dropped onto my hands and knees and crawled through the gap in the canvas and onto the dewy grass. Eve followed close behind.

"Wait," Eve hissed.

I stopped as footsteps padded nearby. Leaves crunched and a tent flap swished. I peered out into the darkness, my heart thumping.

"It's clear," Eve whispered a few moments later, rising to her feet.

I followed her out into the night.

We passed through the sleeping camp, darting from tent to tent. Wood smoke drifted in the air and tent canvas creaked in the wind. We moved when the wind was strongest, using the shaking of the branches to cover our footsteps. I didn't see a soul, but I knew there would be guards posted all around.

"Stay here," Eve told me when we reached a thicket of undergrowth.

I crouched and watched her silently sneak away. Moonlight glinted on the spear tied to her back, then she merged with the dark between the trees. A few moments later, she was back.

"Come on," she said.

We hurried away from the camp, pausing regularly to listen to the sounds of the forest. Every so often we changed direction and several times we seemed to double back on ourselves. Eve led me through the forest without uttering a word. The moon was bright, casting crooked shadows all around us, and we moved so quickly I didn't have a chance to look at the map.

But I didn't need the map to know we were getting close to the Festian Swamps – my nose was accurate enough. I smelled stagnant water and rotting vegetation. The trees around us began to thin. Then

we stepped out into the moonlit expanse
of the swamps.

The water shone like silver, and
herds of sleeping Goretusks snored and
grunted all across the swamp. Eve finally
stopped. Behind her the vast shadow of
Mammoth Peak dominated the sky.

"Thanks," I said, a little out of breath. "For getting me out of the camp."

Eve shrugged.

"I owed you a favor," she said. "And anyway, I want to see if you're right about these magic stones."

I stared at her. She was full of surprises.

"You don't have to take me all that way," I said. "Or go inside the mines. I can get the stones on my own. I've got maps."

I was about to show her the Map of Monsters, but she shook her head and started walking.

"Just follow me," she said. "I don't want you wandering into the swamp and getting stuck again."

"It was a Goretusk," I told her. "A Goretusk pushed me in!"

◂ ◊ △ ◊ ◂

We were nearing the northern edge of the swamps when Eve stopped and peered toward the tree line over to our right.

"Did you hear that?" she said, reaching for her spear.

"What?" I asked.

I stared across the short stretch of swamp that separated us from the forest. I couldn't hear or see anything, so I took the map from my knapsack and opened it up.

Big purple Goretusk lights crowded the swamps behind us. There was another light, too. It was small and amber, and it was darting about at the edge of the trees.

"Don't worry," I said to Eve. "It's nothing dangerous, just a Leatherwing called Starla. She's my friend."

I looked up and found Eve staring at the map in astonishment. She stepped closer and gazed at the colored lights.

"What is this?" she asked, her voice quiet with awe.

"It's the Map of Monsters," I replied. "Each light shows a different creature. That's how I know it's Starla over there in the trees."

Eve touched Starla's amber light with the tip of her finger, then drew it away as if she might be burned. I felt a strange kind

of pride at being entrusted with such a
magical thing.

The light began to move, and I pointed
at the tree line.

"There," I said to Eve.

She looked up just as Starla flapped
out of the trees.

"A Leatherwing," Eve muttered to herself, glancing down at the map once again.

"It's all right, Starla," I called out. "Eve is a friend."

"Are you sure, Leo Wilder?" Starla replied, hovering near the tree line.

It was good to hear her voice echoing round my head again.

"I'm sure," I said. "You're not going to hurt her, are you, Eve?"

Eve shook her head slowly and returned her spear to the holster on her back.

"I hope you're right, Leo Wilder," said Starla, approaching cautiously.

When she was younger, Starla had been tricked by forest people. They trapped her in a cage. Now, she found it difficult to trust them.

"You can trust Eve," I told her. "I promise. She helped me escape from the camp and she wants to help us find the magic stones."

Starla gave me a long, hard stare.

"Well, all right, Leo Wilder," she finally agreed.

She flapped down and landed on my shoulder, but I could tell she was still scared.

Eve watched all this in fascination. It was clear that she had only heard my half of the conversation.

"So it's true," she asked, watching Starla closely, "Leatherwings can speak with their thoughts?"

"It's true," I said.

She raised her eyebrows, clearly impressed.

"We should go," I said, looking north toward the shadow of Mammoth Peak.

"It's not far now," said Eve. "Just past that hill."

She set off along the swamp path and I followed, Starla's tiny claws gripping tight to my shoulder.

"Don't worry," I whispered to Starla. "It'll be all right."

◂ ◊ △ ◊ ▸

The swamps dried up as we reached the base of the hill. It was steep and rocky, and I had to push myself to keep up with Eve. She never seemed to get tired, and her feet never slipped on the loose rocks. I'd slipped over so many times that Starla had given up riding on my shoulder, choosing to fly on ahead instead. I was eager to reach the hilltop and have a rest. But I was also afraid of what was waiting for us there.

Finally, I reached the summit and stopped, wiping the sweat from my face. Down a short slope lay a broad, flat area strewn with rocks. Several enormous,

house-sized boulders lay scattered about, and a vast cliff face rose over it all. I saw Eve scrambling gracefully down the slope and Starla circling high above us. At the base of the cliff, I saw a small square of purest black. This was our destination, the entrance to the Endless Mines.

I clambered down the slope and threaded my way between the rocks and boulders. Eve was waiting for me at the cliff face, and I saw that the entrance to the mines was much larger than I'd thought. The crossbeam was twice as high as the top of any normal door and it was wide enough to drive a horse

and cart through. Starla
swooped down and landed
near the entrance. All three
of us stood in silence for a
moment, staring into
the dark.

"They always told us it was
haunted," Eve said,
a nervous look in
her eyes. "The elders would
tell ghost stories to keep
us from going inside. They

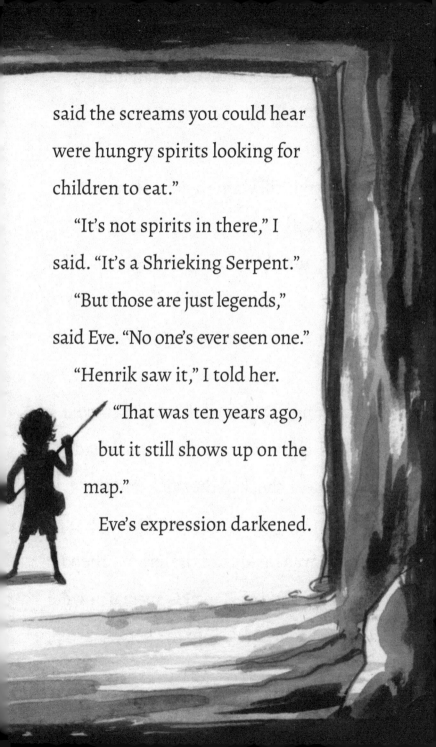

said the screams you could hear were hungry spirits looking for children to eat."

"It's not spirits in there," I said. "It's a Shrieking Serpent."

"But those are just legends," said Eve. "No one's ever seen one."

"Henrik saw it," I told her.

"That was ten years ago, but it still shows up on the map."

Eve's expression darkened.

"Is that better or worse than hungry spirits?" I asked.

"About the same," Eve said.

"Do you still want to go in there with us?" I asked.

Eve paused for a moment, then nodded grimly.

"Someone needs to keep you alive," she said.

I swung my knapsack off and started preparing the lantern that Henrik had given me. I checked the wick and the paraffin and made sure everything I needed was inside the tinderbox. Then I took the bottle of Henrik's special powder and tucked it safely into my pocket. I kept

Henrik's map of the mines in my hand along with the Map of Monsters.

"It smells bad in there, Leo Wilder," said Starla. "And hardly any space for flying. Are you sure the stones are in there? Maybe there's another place you could try first? Like a nice outdoor sort of place?"

"Sorry," I said. "The stones only exist in the mines. You can stay outside and keep watch if you like? We'll be quick. We'll grab the stones and get out."

Starla screwed up her face.

"No way," she said. "We face the monsters together, Leo Wilder. Always."

"All right," I said, smiling.

I lit the lantern and held it up to the darkness of the tunnel. Henrik's polished square of metal sent the lantern light forward in a concentrated beam. I took the bottle of powder from my pocket and sprinkled a tiny pinch onto the flame.

Starla leaped back as the lantern blazed blindingly bright, first white, then orange, red, green, and blue, before dying

down to its normal paraffin name.

"Well, that seems to work," I said. "Are you ready?"

I looked at Starla, then at Eve, and received a nod from each of them. I held the lantern in one hand, the maps in the other, and I led the way into the Endless Mines.

We walked quietly, watching our footing in the lantern light. Each of us knew that silence was the only way we would pass through these tunnels without alerting the Serpent. I glanced back once and saw that the entrance had shrunk to a tiny gray square of moonlit night. Above us, the mountain seemed to hang like a vast stone trap, waiting to be sprung.

The tunnel had been hacked into the rock, with wooden supports jammed into the walls and roof every twenty or thirty paces. I looked for clues about what the mine might have been used for, but all I could see were chunks of rock and rotten wood that had fallen from the walls. Small puddles of water shone in the lamplight, and the tunnels echoed with drips and splashes. The air was cold, damp, and incredibly still.

Soon we reached the first fork in the tunnel and I paused to read Henrik's map. Eve peered over my shoulder.

"Left?" I said.

"It looks like it," she replied.

Starla had already edged forward into the left-hand fork.

I checked the Map of Monsters and saw nothing nearby. A few tiny gray dots were clustered off to the east. They looked like Crag Hounds, and I was pretty sure they lived high up on the outsides of the mountains. There was no sign of the Serpent.

We set off down the next section of tunnel and I began to get used to the darkness. The lantern worked well, and I was glad to have Starla and Eve alongside me.

I scuffed a small stone with my boot, and it skittered away. Starla glanced back at me.

"Quiet, Leo Wilder," she said.

"Sorry," I whispered.

We walked on and the tunnel began to slope gently downward. The air grew colder and we passed the entrance to the first side tunnel. I checked Henrik's map and was confident I knew where we were. Soon after that we reached the second side tunnel. This was the one we needed to take. I paused at the tunnel entrance, double-checking the map. Just a few more twists and turns, and we'd reach the underground river and the waterfall. Then we could get the stones and get out of there. It was going to be all right.

Even as I told myself that, I saw Starla freeze in front of me. She'd walked a few steps beyond the tunnel entrance and her ears were pointing forward, her long body tensed. She'd heard something.

I glanced at Eve and she reached for her spear.

An echo of sound was rolling toward us. It was quiet at first but quickly rose into a deafening, high-pitched shriek.

The Serpent was coming.

SIX

I stared at the Map of Monsters as the shriek died away. The gray, arrow-shaped light of the Serpent had appeared from nowhere and it was heading straight for us.

"How did that happen?" I said. "The tunnels were all clear a minute ago!"

"Maybe that map's not as clever as you thought," said Eve. "Come on!"

She headed into the side tunnel.

"Wait!" I said, fumbling in my pocket for the bottle of Henrik's powder. "We can't outrun it. We need to scare it off with the lantern!"

The bottle of powder slipped from my fingers as I spoke. It fell to the floor, but luckily it didn't break. I crouched to pick it up and Eve glared at me from the edge of the lantern's pool of light.

"You really think that's going to work?" she said. "Your map certainly doesn't. We need to get out of here."

I grabbed the bottle, and my hand shook as I tried to remove the stopper.

A scraping noise began to drift from

the dark of the tunnel.

"It's too late to run," I told Eve.

She glared at me for a moment, then drew her spear.

Up ahead, Starla sniffed the air and flapped from one side of the tunnel to the other. I could tell she was frightened. I was frightened too, but we had no choice. We had to stand our ground.

It emerged from the shadows slowly, a giant snake with eyes the size of dinner plates. Its scales were a pale, grayish yellow and its tongue flickered out between two long, curved fangs.

Starla scrambled away from it with

a cry and for a moment I stood frozen in fear. I watched as the Serpent reared up and opened its jaws. A shriek leaped from its throat, so loud that the sound vibrated through my body and sent me stumbling backward.

Something bright shot past me and I realized that Eve had thrown her spear. It struck the scales of the Serpent's neck and ricocheted harmlessly away.

It was all down to me now. I was the only one who could stop this monster.

"Cover your eyes!" I shouted to Starla and Eve.

I opened the powder bottle with my teeth and shook it over the lantern flame.

The tunnel erupted in blinding white light and I squeezed my eyes shut. The Serpent shrieked again. It was even louder than before and so high-pitched that it hurt my ears. I steadied my feet and held the lantern out before me. Even through my eyelids I could see it burn green then red then brilliant blue.

Another deafening shriek blasted through the tunnel, but as it faded, I heard the frantic slithering of scales on stone.

The lantern light died back to its normal glow and I opened my eyes. The Serpent had fled. Henrik's magic powder had worked.

I glanced at Eve and she stared back at me, as stunned as I was. Starla crouched by the tunnel wall, blinking hard.

"Come on," I said, heading for the side tunnel. "Let's get out of here before it comes back."

"I need my spear," said Eve, peering cautiously into the darkness beyond the lantern's glow.

Starla ran into the shadows and reappeared moments later dragging

Eve's spear in her teeth. She dropped it at Eve's feet.

"Thank you," Eve said, sounding very surprised.

Starla gave her a quick nod, then ran to join me at the junction of the two tunnels.

"Let's go, Leo Wilder," she said.

The new tunnel was much narrower than the main one. It was steeper, too, with thin streams of water trickling over the rocky ground. I took the lead, with Starla scampering close behind and Eve bringing up the rear. There were loose stones everywhere, but I didn't dare slow down.

The tunnel took a sharp turn to the right, then another turn back to the left. It grew even narrower and the roof was so low I could have reached up and touched it. Then I heard a sound.

I stopped.

"What is it?" Eve asked.

Starla ran between my legs and stood a few paces ahead.

"Hissing," I said. "I can hear hissing."

I held the Map of Monsters up to the lantern light. There was no sign of the Serpent, but the map had been wrong before.

"I can hear something, too," said Eve, drawing her spear.

I took the bottle of powder from my pocket, preparing myself for another fight.

"No need for that," said Starla, swishing her tail excitedly. "This isn't hissing, Leo Wilder. This is water!"

She ran on ahead and I followed, still clutching the magic powder just in case. The sound grew louder and there seemed to be a faint glow of light up ahead.

"Do you see that, too?" I called to Eve.

"Light," she said. "But we're underground. Where's it coming from?"

I had no answer. All I could do was keep running.

Starla was so far ahead by now that I couldn't see her anymore. The haze of light had formed itself into a rectangle and the rectangle slowly grew to become an opening of some kind. What I'd thought was a hissing sound now seemed very much like the rushing of water.

Starla's voice echoed in my head:

"Come on, Leo Wilder! Hurry up!"

I ran through the opening and

gasped at the vast space that opened up around me. It was the cavern Henrik had told me about, but it was nothing like I'd imagined. You could have fit half the village inside it, and it rose ten times higher than our protective Village Wall. A river gushed through the center of it all, bursting from a waterfall up high and disappearing into a tunnel at the other end of the cavern. The waterfall gave off a strange silver glow, which cast flickering shadows over the craggy walls and the jumble of huge boulders that made up the cavern floor. This was where the light had been coming from, and I wondered if it had

anything to do with the magic stones.

"This is it," I said to Eve. "The stones should be in a pool below the waterfall."

Eve nodded, staring around the cavern with an awestruck expression.

Then Starla swooped past us.

"I can see the pool!" she called to me. "Come on, Leo Wilder!"

I began clambering over the boulders toward the waterfall. They were smooth and rounded, and I imagined the river filling the whole cavern during the springtime floods. It was tricky finding a safe way through the boulders. The smaller ones shifted and rolled under my weight and there were cracks between the larger ones that I could easily have fallen into. Annoyingly, Eve clambered past me as if all this were no problem at all and a few moments later she had reached the edge of the water.

"I hope you can swim," she said, when I eventually joined her.

I finally realized why Henrik had insisted I learn over the summer.

The pool was almost as big as the market square back home and its waters foamed and swirled with the powerful currents of the river.

I handed the lantern and the magic powder to Eve.

"You only need a small pinch of

powder to make the flame flare up," I told
her. "You'd better have the map, too."

I set my knapsack down and began
taking off my boots. Starla flapped over
and perched next to me.

"I need you to keep watch," I told her.

"The Serpent may not show up on the map, and it looks like there are ways into this cavern all over the place."

Starla looked around at the cavern walls.

"Lots of holes to sneak through," she said. "But don't worry, Leo Wilder. I'll smell that monster if it comes our way."

"Thanks," I said, grateful for Starla's powerful sense of smell. "You'll have to tell Eve if you think the Serpent's coming."

Starla wrinkled her nose. She still hadn't actually spoken to Eve yet.

"All right, Leo Wilder," she said, glancing over at Eve. Instead of looking scared she seemed almost fascinated by the forest girl.

I rummaged inside my knapsack and found the sack Henrik had given me. It had a long strap for carrying and a drawstring to seal it with. This is what I'd use to collect the stones.

"You both know what to do if the Serpent comes?" I asked, slinging the strap of the sack across my back and chest.

"Of course, Leo Wilder," said Starla.

Eve gave me a grim nod as she scanned the shadowy depths of the cavern.

I took a deep breath to steady my nerves. Then I crept to the edge of the pool and climbed down into the dark, swirling waters.

SEVEN

The water was so cold it took my breath away. I clung to the nearest boulder, gasping in shock. But I didn't have time to waste. I knew the Serpent could reappear at any moment, so I pushed off from the boulder and started swimming.

The waterfall roared and the powerful currents of the pool tried to drag me off toward the fast-flowing river. I fought against it, kicking my legs, and splashing furiously with my arms, just like Henrik had showed me.

"I thought you said you could swim," Eve called out in an urgent whisper.

I ignored her and kept going.

My arms were aching already, and

the sack on my back wasn't making things any easier, but I kept swimming through the pool toward the silver glow of the waterfall. I reached the cliff face alongside the waterfall and clung on to the rock, breathing hard and shivering with cold as the cascade of water crashed into the pool beside me.

I looked out across the cavern and saw Starla circling high up in the flickering light. Eve was clambering back across the boulders toward the tunnel entrance, holding the lantern out in front of her. I was glad they were there to watch out for me.

I peered into the water, but the glow

from the waterfall didn't reach very far.
I had no idea how deep the pool was.
All I knew was that the magic stones
were down there and it was my job to
get them. I took a deep, deep breath and
held the air in. Then, without allowing
myself time to think, I dived beneath
the surface.

Swimming straight down was harder than I'd expected, and I was glad Eve couldn't see me as I twisted about clumsily under the water. Luckily, the pool wasn't very deep, and I quickly reached the bottom.

It was too dark to see, but my hands pressed down against a mass of smooth, round pebbles. I grabbed a handful and stuffed them into the sack that was hanging from my chest. I took another handful, then another, then I swam up and gasped air into my lungs as I broke the surface. The sack was half full and it was already making swimming difficult, but I needed more stones. I bobbed up and down in the water, kicking my feet and circling my arms to stay afloat. Then, when I'd caught my breath, I took another deep gulp of air and dived.

I filled the bag and swam back up. By the time I reached the surface I was exhausted, the sack of stones doing its best to pull me back into the depths. I clung to the cliff face, letting the water drip from my face and trickle out of my ears. I was about to set off across the pool when Starla's voice burst into my head like an alarm:

"Leo! Eve!"

I thought how nice it was that Starla was talking to Eve as well now—until I realized why.

"Bring the lantern, Eve!" cried Starla. "Leo, get out of the water! The Serpent is here!" I saw Starla circling frantically near the roof of the cavern.

"Swim, Leo Wilder!" she cried. "Swim!"

A chunk of rock crashed into the water just an arm's length away from me. A spray of gravel rained onto my head and threw up splashes all around me. I looked up.

There was the Serpent, coming for me down the cliff face.

Its scaly body clung to the ledges and cracks. Bits of rock tumbled down as it slithered this way and that, no more than ten

paces above me.

Its big eyes glared at me and it opened its fang-filled mouth.

A terrifying shriek tore through the air.

I leaned into the rock face as the blast of air struck my body. A powerful wave rose up and dragged me from the rock, forcing me to swim for it.

I saw Eve at the edge of the pool raising the lantern, then the waves blocked my view. I swam with all my might, struggling to stay afloat while the bag of stones tried to pull me down. My head sank below the surface and it took all my strength to swim up and gulp down a breath. It was too far. I'd gathered too many stones and I wasn't going to make it.

"Close your eyes, Leo Wilder!" said Starla.

I heard her wings beat the air around my head and felt her tiny paws against my back. She grabbed the strap that was slung across my body and lifted it, hovering over me as she took the weight of the stones.

"Close your eyes!" she said again.

As I rose to the surface, I squeezed my eyes shut and kept swimming, putting all my trust in Starla and Eve.

Even through my eyelids I saw the lantern light flare. The Serpent must have seen it too because it let out another loud shriek.

I heard a huge splash and the shrieking suddenly stopped. Something huge swept past me underwater and I thought I'd be dragged along in its wake. I opened my eyes and saw Eve just a few strokes away. Starla was still with me, her big leathery wings beating the air above my head.

When I reached the edge of the pool, Eve grabbed my hand and helped me climb out onto the rocks. A shriek echoed from somewhere downriver, and I glanced nervously across the cavern.

"It's all right," said Eve. "It got swept away. I saw it swim out of the cavern!"

I collapsed onto my back and smiled. Then I thanked Starla for saving my life.

"Well, it was both of us, really,"
Starla replied. "Eve helped a little bit.
But anyway, we should get out of these
horrible mines, Leo Wilder."

"That sounds like a great idea," I said.

I stowed the magic stones in my
knapsack and put my boots on, then we
set off back into the tunnels.

Eve led the way with the lantern
and Starla followed close behind, half
running and half flying. I heaved myself
after them, dripping wet and freezing.
We raced through the echoing mines,
gradually climbing from the depths.
There was no sign of the Serpent on
the map, and we didn't hear its shriek

again. Even so, none of us wanted to
hang around and we soon emerged
into the cool night air of the hillside,
breathless and relieved.

"We did it, Leo Wilder! We did it!" said Starla, flapping about victoriously.

I grinned.

"We did, didn't we," I said.

I looked over at Eve and she allowed herself a smile, too.

"Thanks," I said, giving her a hug. "We couldn't have done it without you."

She hugged me back awkwardly.

"We should get you home," she said. "It's almost morning."

I looked out across the forest and saw that Eve was right. The sky was beginning to lighten in the east.

"Let's go," I agreed, knowing Mum would be worried about me.

We hurried down the rocky hillside and passed around the edge of the Festian Swamps, wrinkling our noses at the boggy stench. The herds of Armored Goretusks snored and grunted as they slept, their hard, mossy backs gently rising and falling in the rippling water.

Soon we reached the forest. The wind had died down and it was eerily quiet. We found the river path and I squelched along briskly in my wet clothes, eager to get home. It was still dark among the trees and when I looked around me, I kept expecting to see the Serpent's huge eyes peering back. I couldn't quite believe we'd gone all the way to the

Endless Mines and gotten the better of the Shrieking Serpent. The weight of the stones in my knapsack made me feel proud. I felt proud of my friends, too. And very lucky to have them. Without Starla and Eve I would never have made it through the mines.

We reached a part of the river that I recognized, and I stopped, swinging my knapsack from my shoulders.

"We can make our own way back from here," I said to Eve, who stopped a few paces ahead of me. "Thanks for everything. I hope you don't get in too much trouble for helping me escape from your camp."

Eve shrugged.

"I'll be all right," she said. "I might have to steer clear of Wynter for a while, though."

I reached into the sack of stones and drew out a handful.

"Here," I said. "Take these."

She gave me a surprised look, then held out her hands.

"I'm not sure which stones they are," I said. "So be careful."

Starla flapped over and sniffed at the stones in Eve's palm.

"You have a vine-stone, two stink-stones, and a lightning-stone," she said, separating them as she spoke.

"You can have some more if you like?" I said to Eve, but she shook her head.

"Thanks," she said. "But this is more than enough."

She studied the stones in her palm, holding them ever so carefully, as if she were afraid of what they might do.

"I recommend a stink-stone in Wynter's tent if she gives you any trouble," I said.

Eve smiled and took a small pouch from her belt. She slipped the stones inside and thanked me again.

"Maybe I could show you how they work some time?" I said. "And you could show me how to walk more quietly in the forest, or use a spear?"

"I'd like that," Eve said. "I guess we know where to find each other?"

We said our goodbyes and began walking in opposite directions along the river path. Starla flew beside me, but before I'd walked more than a few paces she swung around and flew back to Eve. I saw a smile cross Eve's face and I knew Starla had said something that only Eve could hear.

"Thank you," Eve replied. "I hope so too."

EIGHT

The Green River flowed calmly beside me as I walked. Moonlight made the path easy to follow and the sky grew gradually lighter.

Starla flew a short way ahead. She was the first to spot the old wooden bridge that led toward the village.

"Here it is, Leo Wilder," she said.

She swooped down and perched on a

tree stump beside the bridge. Her wings drooped with exhaustion and I realized how difficult this mission must have been for her. She'd overcome her fears and accepted Eve—and she'd traveled underground to face the Serpent. The mines were a scary place for me, but Starla was used to flying through the open sky, so it had probably been even worse for her.

"You were really brave today," I said. "I couldn't have gotten those stones without you. I probably would have drowned, too."

Starla smiled proudly.

"And thanks for being kind to Eve," I said. "I know that wasn't easy."

"If Eve is also your friend," said Starla,

"then I suppose she can be my friend too."

I smiled back. It made me very glad to hear her say that.

"I need to get these stones to Henrik," I said. "Then I need to sleep."

"Me too," said Starla. "The sleeping part, that is!"

She flapped into the air.

"See you next time, Leo Wilder!" she said. "But no more mines, please!"

"No more mines," I agreed as she flew off toward the trees.

I skirted round the edge of the village and made my way to Henrik's cabin. The windows flickered with light and the door creaked open before I reached it.

"Is that you, boy?" Henrik growled.

"It's me," I said.

Henrik smiled and I could see the relief in his eyes. As I entered the cabin, he looked me up and down, as if he was checking that all my limbs were still attached.

I dumped my knapsack on his desk and the stony clank made him raise his eyebrows expectantly.

"You got them?" he murmured. "Good lad. Good lad."

I pulled out the sack and Henrik examined its contents as I unloaded the lantern, maps, and magic powder.

"Hmm," he said, nodding as he held

a stone up to the light. "And did you see the Shrieking Serpent?" he asked. "Did it cause you any trouble?"

"You could say that," I muttered.

I told him what had happened: getting stuck in the Festian Swamps, my imprisonment and escape from the forest people camp, our descent into the mines, and our battles with the Serpent.

Henrik's brows grew increasingly furrowed.

"You took a forest girl with you into the mines?" he asked. "I thought I told you not to trust them. You know they don't take kindly to villagers."

"Eve must be different, then," I said. "She set me free from the camp and helped me and Starla the whole time. We would never have gotten the stones without her."

"Well," Henrik grumbled, "I hope you don't come to regret it, boy. It could cause us a lot of trouble. It could cause the forest people trouble, too."

I decided not to tell him that I'd given Eve a handful of stones.

"At least you made it back safe," he said. "And you got us our stones. So I suppose it doesn't matter how you did it. Let me find you some dry clothes, lad. Then you'd better get on home."

◂ ◊ △ ◊ ▸

I crept through the secret door in the Village Wall and hurried toward home. Dawn had broken and a few hardworking villagers were already out in the streets. I wondered if Mum and Lulu had waited up all night for me, and when I reached

the back door and slipped inside, I
stopped for a moment in the kitchen. A
fire was still blazing in the living room.
I could hear Mum sorting through her
work papers and the slow creak of Lulu's
rocking chair. I took a deep breath, made
sure I had my cover story straight, then I
went through.

"Leo!" Mum cried, sitting upright in
her sickbed.

Lulu jumped out of her chair and sent
Stickle the cat leaping angrily away.

"I'm sorry," I said quickly. "I wasn't
supposed to be out this late, but I was
working on the riverbank and I fell in and
then the river dragged me away and when

I managed to get out, I was a really long way from the village, and it was dark, so I found a hollow tree and I hid there until it started getting light . . ."

"Come here," said Mum, stretching her arms toward me.

I went over and she grabbed me into a hug.

"Gilda said you'd be out late, but when you didn't come home we were all so worried," she said, squeezing me tight. "Your sister's been to the Village Hall twice and Gilda was about to send out a search party."

She let me go and looked at the baggy shirt and trousers Henrik had given me.

"Well, at least they gave you some dry clothes," she said.

My legs felt like they were about to give up completely, so I dropped into a chair beside the fire.

Lulu shook her head and laughed.

"You fell in the river?" she said. "That's clumsy, even for you."

She got up from her rocking chair.

"I'll get you a drink," she said, and fetched me a mug of hot tea from the kitchen.

"Thanks," I said, feeling awkward and silly and wishing more than ever that I could tell Mum and Lulu what had actually happened.

Mum reached over and placed a hand on my shoulder as I drank my tea.

"We're just glad you're all right," she said. "Now you finish that tea and get off to bed. No work for you today. I'll make sure Gilda knows you won't be going out on your Assignment. Lulu, maybe you could deliver these accounts to the Grimwoods?"

I'd forgotten all about the paperwork I was supposed to take to the Grimwood house. Usually, hearing that name was enough to fill me with dread, but somehow it didn't seem so bad anymore. I thought of Carl Grimwood, the worst bully in the village, and I found that I wasn't scared at all.

"It's all right," I said. "I'll take them round."

Lulu frowned at me. She knew what Carl was like.

"Really," I said. "It's fine. I'll have a good nap, then I'll deliver the accounts like I said."

Mum raised her eyebrows.

"Well, if you're sure?" she asked.

"I'm sure," I said, taking a slurp of the delicious hot tea.

After the Shrieking Serpent and the Endless Mines, Carl Grimwood was nothing much to worry about.

Plus, I had a stink-stone in my pocket just in case.

THE ARMORED GORETUSK

STRENGTH	10	MONSTER TYPE
SIZE	9	Swamp Monster
SPEED	7	HABITAT
INTELLIGENCE	4	Festian Swamps
WEAPONRY	8	FOOD

MONSTER TYPE
Swamp Monster

HABITAT
Festian Swamps

FOOD
Bog-weed, low shrubs, and leaf mulch

ATTACK STYLE

The Armored Goretusk is herbivorous, but will charge when provoked, using its considerable weight and its four long, curved tusks to destroy or impale anything in its path.

DESCRIPTION

A large, four-legged monster with an armor-plated back and four irregular tusks. Young Goretusks can measure up to six paces in length and three in height. Adult Goretusks can be up to twenty-five paces long. The armor plating on a Goretusk's back provides protection from predators and is often covered with moss and other vegetation. Goretusks rarely leave their swamp habitat, preferring to wallow in the water in herds, feasting on the foul-smelling bog-weed that lies just below the surface.

THE LEATHER-WING

STRENGTH	2
SIZE	2
SPEED	9
INTELLIGENCE	10
WEAPONRY	4

MONSTER TYPE
Desert Monster

HABITAT
Clay Desert

FOOD
Insects and fruit

ATTACK STYLE

Though small, Leatherwings can be ferocious, and will use their sharp teeth and claws to fend off predators. Their agility in the air makes them very successful insect hunters.

DESCRIPTION

The Leatherwing is a small, furry, four-legged creature that flies using its oversize, featherless wings. Leatherwings live together in large families, or "clan groups," traveling across the vast Clay Desert in search of seasonal feeding grounds. Leatherwing clan groups often build temporary burrows in the walls of ravines, their sand-colored fur providing highly efficient camouflage.

STRENGTH	9
SIZE	8
SPEED	8
INTELLIGENCE	9
WEAPONRY	9

MONSTER TYPE
Rock Monster

HABITAT
Tunnels and caves

DIET
Anything that moves

DESCRIPTION

A giant snake that lives and hunts underground—so rare that many people think it's nothing but a myth. The Serpent's sight and hearing are incredibly sensitive, and nothing passes through its domain unnoticed. Its deafening, high-pitched shrieks are truly terrifying, and, like a bat, it uses the echoes from these shrieks to hunt down intruders.

ATTACK STYLE

Once the Serpent locates its prey, it slithers through the dark at high speed, ready to gulp it down in a single bite.

THE STONES

STINK-STONE

FIRE-STONE

SLEEP-STONE

VANISH-STONE

FLOOD-STONE

LIGHTNING-STONE

SCREECH-STONE

VINE-STONE

SHRINK-STONE

CHOOSE YOUR STONES
WISELY . . .

ABOUT THE AUTHOR

KRIS HUMPHREY

Kris has done his fair share of interesting jobs (cinema projectionist, blood factory technician, bookseller, teacher). But he's always been writing—or at least thinking about writing.

In 2012 Kris graduated with distinction from the MA in Writing for Young People at Bath Spa University, winning the award for Most Promising Writer. He is the author of two series of books for young readers: *Guardians of the Wild* and now, *Leo's Map of Monsters*.

PETE WILLIAMSON

Read all of Leo's incredible adventures!